Flora and the Flames

Written by Jane Lawes

Illustrated by Alexandra Badiu

Collins

Chapter 1

"COME ON!" Flora shouted at the TV. Her favourite basketball team, the Shooting Stars, were playing against their biggest rivals and the score was even with only 30 seconds to go.

The captain of the Shooting Stars dribbled
the ball down the court towards the hoop, and
Flora held her breath as the ball flew up and sailed
through the net with a whoosh.

"Yes!" Flora shouted as the whistle blew for
the end of the game –
the Shooting Stars had won!

A homework diary landed on the table in front of Flora, breaking her out of her memory of last night's game. She smiled shyly at the girl who had given it to her – Ms Thompson had said her name was Chloe. Chloe smiled back and sat down next to Flora. She took her pencil case out of her bag and Flora saw that it had the Shooting Stars logo on it.

"Did you watch the game last night?" Flora asked excitedly.

"Yes!" said Chloe. "The end was amazing."

"Quiet, please!" Ms Thompson called. She went through all the usual start-of-the-year things, which Flora listened to carefully because she was new.

Finally, Ms Thompson told them that she'd be choosing the Year Six basketball team at the end of the week. "Our first match is only three weeks away," said Ms Thompson. "And it's against Meadowlands!" A worried murmur rippled around the classroom.

"They're our biggest rivals," Chloe whispered to Flora. "We've never beaten them."

Flora looked around the room. At her old school, she'd been the best in her year at basketball, but there might be children here who were better than her. She made up her mind to practise more than ever when she got home, to give herself the best chance she could.

Chapter 2

Dad had put up a basketball hoop for Flora as soon as they'd moved in, and she practised shooting the ball towards it after school.

"Nice shot!" a voice said, just as the ball whooshed through the net.

Flora spun around and saw a girl sitting on the wall between her garden and her neighbour's.

"I'm Tahlia," the girl said. "What school do you go to?"

"I just started at Frampton Primary," Flora answered.

Tahlia laughed. "Even a basketball player as good as you won't help Frampton win," she said. "I'm on the Meadowlands team and we beat you every year. Frampton are rubbish."

"Not this year!" Flora shot back.

Tahlia just laughed and hopped down off the wall into her own garden.

Flora practised basketball every day after school, trying to ignore Tahlia whenever she popped up on the wall to watch and laugh every time Flora missed a shot.

On Friday, Flora's class played basketball in PE. Ms Thompson was going to choose the team at the end of the lesson, so Flora played with all the determination she had.

She was on the same team as Chloe, and between them, they scored so many points that Flora thought Tahlia must be lying about Frampton being rubbish.

It felt wonderful! She loved running down
the court, dribbling the ball and feeling the cool
September air rush against her cheeks, and she
loved the thrill of watching the ball fly from her
hands and into the net.

When she grew up, she wanted to be just like the Shooting Stars, playing for a real basketball team, winning competitions and trophies and playing all around the world. She was disappointed when the game was over and everyone trooped back to the classroom.

Just before the end of the day, Ms Thompson announced the basketball team. Flora's name was called first, and then Chloe's. Flora tried to pay attention to the other players who were chosen but she didn't know everyone's name yet, and anyway, she and Chloe were too busy grinning at each other.

"Maybe with a player like you on the team, we can finally beat Meadowlands!" Chloe said.

Flora smiled. But she knew that it took more than one good player to make a great team.

Chapter 3

Chloe invited Flora and the rest of the team to go bowling on Sunday so that Flora could get to know everyone before the big match.

"The girl next door to me is on the team at Meadowlands," Flora said, while they put on their bowling shoes.

"What's she like?" Aisha asked.

Flora told them what Tahlia had said, and how mean she'd been every time Flora had seen her.

"We'll prove her wrong," Max said.

"Yeah!" agreed Ben. "This year, she'll see we're not rubbish. We're going to win."

Flora grinned. Tahlia had no idea what was coming.

In Monday's PE lesson, the basketball team had their first practice together. Flora was excited about playing with her new teammates for the first time. She couldn't wait to feel the rush of joy she'd experienced in Friday's PE lesson again.

But it didn't come. Passes went wrong, the classmates they were playing against intercepted the ball any time Flora or her teammates got close to the hoop, and Ben, who was playing in defence for Flora's team, couldn't stop the other team scoring points.
They lost the game.

"How are we going to beat Meadowlands?" asked Aisha. "We can't even beat our own classmates."

"We've still got two weeks to practise," said Chloe. "We can get better. Right, Flora?"

Two weeks to turn a rubbish team into one that could beat Meadowlands – could it be done? Maybe, if they practised every day for the next two weeks, they might have a chance.

Flora nodded. "Yes," she said. "We can do it!"

Chapter 4

That night, Flora searched the internet for basketball drills. She wrote them down in a notebook and brought it to school the next day. Chloe asked Ms Thompson if they could use some of the basketballs at lunchtime, and they all met in the playground.

Flora explained the first drill, which would help them get better at passing the ball to each other, and soon they were all running up and down the playground, passing basketballs between them.

They did the same thing on Wednesday, and on Thursday, and Flora started to think that her plan might be working. They were improving!

At lunchtime on Friday, Flora went out to their usual meeting place, but no one else was there. She spotted Chloe, Aisha, Ben and Max sitting together in a corner of the playground and went over to them.

"Aren't you coming to practise?" Flora asked.

"Let's have the day off," said Chloe.

"But the match against Meadowlands is next week!" said Flora. "We need to keep training if we want to win."

"We've been training all week," protested Max. "It's boring!"

"That's what it takes to be a great basketball player," said Flora.

"I don't want to be a basketball player!" said Aisha. "I just want to play for fun."

"If we win, it will be fun," Flora insisted.

"*You* go off and train if you care so much about winning," snapped Ben. "We're sick of it."

Flora turned and
ran off to another part
of the playground.
Even Chloe didn't want to
train with her anymore.
Flora felt like crying.

At the end of the day,
she trudged home,
wondering where she'd
gone wrong. She'd only
been doing what she
thought was best for
the team. It had felt so
wonderful to have friends
at her new school already,
but now she'd lost them.

As usual, she practised
shooting hoops in
the garden, but without
her friends, it just didn't
feel the same. She let
the ball roll away and
went inside.

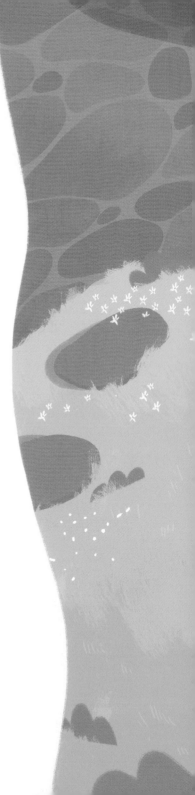

Chapter 5

Flora tried to cheer herself up by watching videos of the Shooting Stars playing basketball on the internet. They looked like they were having such a good time. When they spoke to the camera, they talked about how much they loved being Shooting Stars, how their teammates were their friends and they had fun training together.

Suddenly, Flora had an idea. She grabbed her mobile phone and sent a message to Chloe asking her to come over the next day.

When Chloe arrived on Saturday morning, Flora showed her the videos she'd watched.

"Look, they've made training *fun*!" said Flora.

"We could do that too," said Chloe.

"I was thinking," continued Flora. "What if we had a team name? To make everyone feel like we're part of something special."

"Great idea!" said Chloe.

It didn't take them long to come up with the perfect name: the Frampton Flames. Flora got out a friendship bracelet kit and they spent the next hour making bracelets for everyone on the team with red, orange and yellow beads to represent flames.

"I can't wait to give these to the others," Flora said when they were finished.

"Me neither," said Chloe. "I'm sorry we were mean to you on Friday."

"I'm sorry too," said Flora. "I didn't mean to ruin basketball for everyone."

"Not possible!" said Chloe.

They spent the rest of the morning making up basketball training games in the garden. After a while, Tahlia appeared on the wall to laugh at them and sneer every time one of them missed a shot.

"Ignore her," Chloe said, putting her arm around Flora. "We're going to prove her wrong."

"I hope so," said Flora. But the match was in five days, and they still had a lot to work on.

Chapter 6

Flora felt nervous when she arrived at school on Monday morning. She'd made up with Chloe, but what if the rest of the team still didn't want to be friends?

Chloe gathered the team together in a corner of the classroom. "Flora had a great idea at the weekend," Chloe announced.

"We thought of a name for our team," said Flora. "The Frampton Flames!"

"And we made team bracelets for everyone," added Chloe. Flora handed them out.

"This is awesome!" said Aisha, putting hers on straight away.

"I love the name," said Max.

"Watch out Meadowlands, the Frampton Flames are coming!" said Ben.

They all grinned at each other, and Flora knew they were friends again.

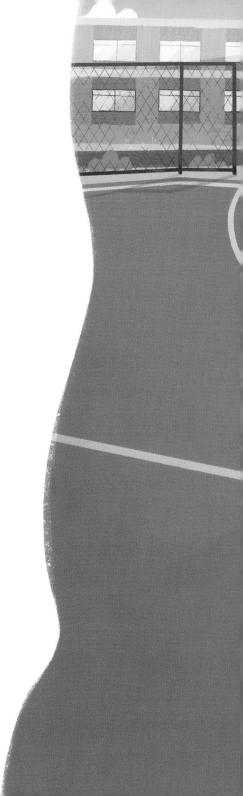

"If we want to beat Meadowlands, we need to get back to training," said Chloe. "Flora and I made up some fun games yesterday – let's try them at lunchtime!"

The others all agreed, and Flora sat down for the first lesson of the day feeling much better than she had all weekend.

When lunchtime came, they ran out to the playground and got to work. Flora and Chloe explained the games they'd made up, and soon everyone was trying them.

34

"Can I lead tomorrow's training?" Aisha asked afterwards. "I've thought of some great ideas for games already."

Flora grinned at Chloe. This just might work.

Aisha led the training session on Tuesday, Max had a turn on Wednesday, and on Thursday, Ben led the games that would get them ready for the match against Meadowlands. They'd been playing basketball in PE too and Flora was starting to feel hopeful – they had definitely got better. But had they improved enough to win?

Chapter 7

After school on Friday, the Meadowlands team arrived with their teacher, and Tahlia led her team out onto the basketball court. Flora took up her starting position nervously and Ms Thompson blew the whistle for the match to begin.

The first three-quarters of the game flew by
in a blur of passes, points missed, points scored,
cheers and sighs of frustration. The more points
the Flames scored, the more Tahlia glared at
Flora, and the more Flora felt her courage rising.
By the end of the third quarter, the score was even.

Flora sank onto the bench that had been placed
at the side of the court, exhausted but happy.
All around her, the Flames were chatting excitedly.
Flora looked across at the Meadowlands bench.
They were sitting in silence, their
expressions glum. They didn't look like they were
friends at all. Flora realised that,
win or lose, she'd much rather be
one of the Flames than on
Tahlia's team.

Having fun with her friends was more important than winning.

Soon it was time to get back onto the court and finish the game. Flora jogged back to her place, feeling calmer now that she knew she wouldn't mind if they lost.

The whistle blew and Max began dribbling the ball down the court. Flora cheered him on, but the ball was soon lost to Tahlia, and they were all running back the other way.

Meadowlands scored, but then Aisha scored for the Flames, keeping the points even.

It stayed that way until there was only one minute left to play, and suddenly, Chloe intercepted the ball and Flora found herself in the perfect position to score. Chloe passed to her, and as soon as the ball reached her hands, Flora aimed it with all her might towards the hoop. She watched it soar up, up, and then down at the exact right moment to swoosh through the net. The whistle blew. The Flames had won!

43

Everyone was cheering and hugging Flora
at once. "Flames forever!" she shouted.

Tahlia stormed off the court, her
face thunderous. Flora turned back to her friends
and carried on celebrating.

Later, when the Flames were on their way
to Chloe's house with their bags packed for
a sleepover, Chloe linked her arm through Flora's.

"This should be our new tradition," said Chloe.
"Win or lose, a sleepover after every match!"

"Whoever we're playing next better get ready,"
said Flora. "The Frampton Flames are coming!"

Olympic Dreams TV

"I'm coming to you live from the basketball court where Team GB have just won their first ever Olympic gold medal for basketball. Here with me is team captain Flora. How long have you been dreaming of this day?"

"It began when I started at a new school and joined the basketball team. My neighbour played for our biggest rivals, and she was really horrible to me. Luckily, my new teammates stood up for me and said we'd win the match and prove Tahlia wrong."

"And did you?"

"Well … it wasn't that simple. Our team wasn't very good, so I got a bit carried away and wore everyone out with practising every day. We all fell out, and that's when I realised that friendship is more important than winning. I'm so lucky to have such great friends playing alongside me for Team GB now."

"But what happened in your school match?"

"My friend Chloe and I came up with a team name and games to make training more fun. We practised a lot, but we had so much fun it didn't feel like hard work. We won the game, and ever since then, I've always remembered what I love most about basketball: that playing makes me feel happy."

"Congratulations on your gold medal!"

"What's that loud ringing sound?"

"That's your alarm clock. Time to wake up for school, Flora!"

 Ideas for reading

Written by Gill Matthews
Primary Literacy Consultant

Reading objectives:
- check that the text makes sense to them, discussing their understanding and explaining the meaning of words in context
- draw inferences such as inferring characters' feelings, thoughts and motives from their actions, and justifying inferences with evidence
- predict what might happen from details stated and implied
- identify how language, structure, and presentation contribute to meaning

Spoken language objectives:
- articulate and justify answers, arguments and opinions
- give well-structured descriptions, explanations and narratives for different purposes, including for expressing feelings
- participate in discussions, presentations, performances, role play, improvisations and debates

Curriculum links: Physical Education

Interest words: nervously, frustration, excitedly, glum, calmer, thunderous

Build a context for reading

- Ask children to look closely at the front cover of the book and to predict what they think it might be about. Who, or what, do they think the *Flames* are?
- Read the blurb. Explore what children know about basketball. What can children infer about Flora from the covers of the book?
- Focus on the fact that this is a contemporary story. What features do the children expect to find in the story?

Understand and apply reading strategies

- Read pp2–7 aloud, using appropriate expression. Ask children what they now know about Flora.
- Discuss any clues in Chapter 1 that tell the reader this is a contemporary story.